Hans Christian Andersen

THE UGLY DUCKLING

Illustrations by Kennedy

BARRON'S

New York/London/Toronto/Sydney

It was summertime. The warm sun shone on an old castle surrounded by a deep moat. From the castle wall all the way down to the water, tall reeds grew. Under the reeds it was like being in the heart of a dense forest. Here, sheltered from the sun, a mother duck sat on her nest, hatching her eggs.

At last, after days of waiting, the eggs began to crack. "Cheep, cheep!" called the ducklings as they poked their little heads out, one after another.

"Quack, quack," answered their mother. And the little ones scurried out of the nest and began to look all around among the green leaves.

"How big the world is!" the ducklings cried. Indeed, they had had very little space to move about inside their eggshells.

"Is everyone here?" asked the mother duck. She got up and looked. But the biggest egg was still lying in the nest, and it gave no sign of cracking. "How long will this take?" the mother duck sighed. And she sat back down on her nest.

An old duck came along to visit the mother duck. "Well, how is it going?" she asked.

"This one is taking such a long time! The shell simply will not crack!" answered the duck on her nest.

"Let's take a look at the egg that won't hatch," said the old duck. "I'll bet it's a turkey's egg. That happened to me once, too. What a pity! Don't waste your time on it. Teach your other little ones to swim."

But the mother continued to sit on the nest. Finally, the last egg hatched, and out tumbled the duckling. "My, but he's large!" the mother exclaimed. "Can he be a turkey chick after all?"

The next day was glorious, with the sun shining brightly on the green leaves. The mother duck took her whole family down to the moat. Splash! Into the water she sprang. And one after another, the ducklings followed her. The water went over their heads, but they bobbed up again and began to swim. Even the big ugly duckling swam with the others.

"No, that's no turkey," said the mother. "He is my own chick after all. And he's really quite handsome when you look at him properly. Quack, quack!"

Then she turned to her children and said, "Come, now, and learn about the world. I will introduce you to the barnyard. But stay close to me, and watch out for the cat!"

They went into the barnyard. "Now, use your legs," the mother duck said. Then she added, "Be sure to bend your necks to the old duck over there. She is the grandest of us all. Do you see? She has a red ribbon tied around her leg. That is the greatest honor a duck can have. It means that she will never be gotten rid of. She is worthy of recognition both by beasts and men. Quack, quack!"

The mother duck continued her lesson. "A well brought up little duck keeps his legs wide apart and his toes turned out. See how I do it? Now, bend your necks and say, 'Quack, quack!'" And they did as she showed them. But the other ducks 'round about looked at them and said, quite loudly, "Oh, dear, see how ugly that big duckling is. We can't have that in our barnyard!"

"Let him be," said the mother. "He is doing no harm."

"What pretty children you have, my dear," said the old duck with the ribbon around her leg. "They are all good-looking except this one."

The mother answered, "He's not handsome, but he is good-natured, and he swims beautifully—perhaps even a bit better than the others. I think he'll improve as he grows up. He was too long in the egg, that's why he doesn't look quite right."

But the poor duckling was pecked and pushed and teased by the ducks and chickens alike. "He's so big and gawky!" they clucked. The turkey, who was born with spurs on and imagined that he was quite an emperor, spread his tail and gobbled furiously until he was red in the face.

The poor duckling didn't know which way to turn. He was in despair because he was so ugly. He was the laughingstock of the whole barnyard.

So the first day passed, and after that matters grew worse and worse. The poor duckling was chased by everyone. His own brothers and sisters teased him, and even his mother wished he were miles away.

The ducks bit him, the hens pecked him, and the farm girl who fed the poultry kicked him aside.

Finally the duckling could stand no more and ran away. Over the hedge he fluttered, frightening the little birds who lived there. "That's because I'm so ugly," he thought. He kept running until he came to the great marsh where the wild ducks lived. He was so tired and miserable that he stayed there all night.

In the morning, the wild ducks flew over to inspect their new comrade. "What sort of creature are you?" they asked. The duckling turned from side to side and greeted them as well as he could.

"You are frightfully ugly," said the ducks. "But that doesn't matter to us, as long as you don't marry into our family." Poor little duckling! He had not thought of marriage. All he wanted was to be allowed to lie among the rushes and sip a little of the marsh water.

After the duckling had been in the marsh for two days, two wild geese found him. "Say, you're so ugly we've taken a fancy to you. Would you like to come with us? Not far away there's another marsh where some charming lady geese live. Perhaps you could find happiness there."

Bang, bang! In that instant two shots rang out. The two geese fell dead among the reeds, and the whole flock of ducks and geese rose from the marsh. It was the beginning of a great hunt. The hunters were hidden all around the marsh, while their dogs wandered about in the swamp—splash, splash! The rushes and reeds fell on all sides.

How frightened the poor ugly duckling was! He twisted around to bury his head under his wing. But just at that moment, he came face to face with a huge, terrible dog. Its tongue hung out hungrily, and its wicked eyes glared like glowing coals.

The fearsome dog came closer and closer to the duckling. "I'm so ugly, even the dog wouldn't bite me!" And he lay there quite still while the buckshot whistled through the reeds.

Later in the day, when all was quiet, the poor little fellow hurried away from the marsh as fast as he could. He ran and ran across fields and meadows, but there was such a strong wind blowing that it was hard for him to make his way. Toward evening, he reached a poor little cottage. The wind was so fierce that the duckling decided to enter in search of shelter.

It was the house of an old woman, who lived there with her cat and her hen.

"What on earth is that?" said the old woman, looking around. But her sight wasn't very good, and she thought the duckling was a fat duck. "Good! Now I can have duck's eggs, if only it isn't a drake!" she exclaimed. And so the duckling was invited to stay, in the expectation that he would lay eggs.

The duckling sat in a corner, quite out of spirits. Suddenly he remembered the fresh air and the sunshine. Then he got such a longing to paddle about on the water that he couldn't help telling the hen about it.

"What possesses you?" exclaimed the hen. "You have nothing to do, that is why you have these strange ideas. Lay some eggs, or start purring. Then you'll get over it!"

"But it's so delightful to swim and dive. You just don't understand me," the duckling said with a sigh.

"Don't moan! Be grateful that you are well sheltered in this house," said the hen.

Feeling greatly misunderstood, the duckling left the cottage to go out a-wandering in the wide world.

Now autumn set in. The leaves in the woods turned yellow and brown, and the wind seized them and whirled them about. It grew colder and colder. In the sky, the clouds hung heavy with the promise of snow and hail. It was a hard time for the poor ugly duckling!

One evening, just as the sun was setting in wintry splendor, a flock of beautiful birds flew out of the marsh. The ugly duckling had never seen such beautiful birds, all dazzlingly white with long, graceful necks. They were swans.

Spreading their magnificent wings, the swans flew away from the cold regions to warmer lands far away.

The ugly duckling felt a strange attraction to the swans. He watched them climb higher and higher until they were out of sight. Time passed, but he could not forget those beautiful birds. He did not know what they were, or where they were going, but he loved them more than anything in the world.

What a cold winter that one was! It grew so cold the duckling had to swim around and around to keep the water from freezing over.

One night he was so weary he stopped swimming, and he became frozen fast into the ice. The next morning, a peasant came along and saw the duckling. He hammered a hole in the ice with his shoe, and carried the duckling home with him.

The peasant's children wanted to play with the duckling. But he was frightened, thinking they were going to tease him. He jumped into the milk pail, splashing milk everywhere. Next, still more frightened, he jumped into the flour sack. Then, frightened more than ever, he jumped out and ran all around the room.

What a sight he was! The peasant's wife clapped her hands and chased him, and the children jumped around, screaming with laughter. Finally the duckling found the open door and escaped from the house.

Once again the duckling was alone. But it would be too sad to tell all the misery he endured during that long, hard winter. He was sheltering among the reeds at the edge of the marsh when the sun began to shine warmly again. The larks were singing, and the beautiful spring had finally come.

The duckling raised his wings and flew until he came to a beautiful garden crossed by brooks and canals. The apple trees were in full bloom, and the air was scented with lilacs.

And there, straight before him, three beautiful swans came floating out from a thicket. They swam majestically over the water, their feathers ruffling lightly in the warm breeze. The duckling recognized the splendid birds and was filled with a desire to fly near them.

"They will put me to death for daring to approach them, because I am so ugly," he thought. He flew to the water and swam toward the white swans. They came to meet him with their wings raised.

"Yes, kill me!" murmured the poor creature, and he bowed his head toward the water. But what did he see reflected there? He saw his own image. And it was not the image of an ugly duckling, but that of a beautiful swan.

Now he was perfectly happy. The big swans swam around him and stroked him with their bills.

Some little children came into the garden and threw corn and bread into the water.

The smallest one cried out, "There's a new one!"

And the other children all exclaimed, "The new one is the most beautiful of all!"

The old swans bowed down before him. Now he felt quite shy, and he hid his head under his wing.

He was blissfully happy, but not at all proud, for a good heart never becomes proud. He thought of how he had once been pursued and scorned, and how he now heard everyone say that he was the most beautiful of all beautiful birds. The sun shone brightly, caressing his slender neck. Deep in his heart, he thought, "I never dreamed of so much happiness when I was the Ugly Duckling!"